'DISPATCH THE MAIMED, THE OLD, THE WEAK, DESTROY THE VERY WORLD ITSELF, FOR WHAT IS THE POINT OF LIFE IF THE PROMISE OF FULFILMENT LIES ELSEWHERE?'

DAPHNE DU MAURIER
Born 1907, London, England
Died 1989, Cornwall, England

'The Breakthrough' was first published in 1966.

DU MAURIER IN PENGUIN MODERN CLASSICS
Don't Look Now and Other Stories

DAPHNE DU MAURIER

The Breakthrough

PENGUIN BOOKS

PENGUIN CLASSICS

UK | USA | Canada | Ireland | Australia
India | New Zealand | South Africa

Penguin Books is part of the Penguin Random House group
of companies whose addresses can be found at
global.penguinrandomhouse.com.

Penguin
Random House
UK

This edition first published 2018
003

Set in 10.25/12.75 pt Dante MT Std
Typeset by Jouve (UK), Milton Keynes
Printed in Great Britain by Clays Ltd, St Ives plc

ISBN: 978-0-241-33920-6

www.greenpenguin.co.uk

MIX
Paper from
responsible sources
FSC® C018179

Penguin Random House is committed to a
sustainable future for our business, our readers
and our planet. This book is made from Forest
Stewardship Council® certified paper.

The Breakthrough

My part in the affair started on September 18th, when my chief
sent for me and told me he was transferring me to Saxmere
on the east coast. He was sorry about it, he said, but I was
the only one with the necessary technical qualifications for
the particular work they had on hand. No, he couldn't give
me any details; they were an odd lot down there, and shut
themselves up behind barbed wire at the slightest provocation.
The place had been a radar experimental station a few years
back, but this was finished, and any experiments that were
going on now were of an entirely different nature, something
to do with vibrations and the pitch of sound.

'I'll be perfectly frank with you,' said my chief, removing
his horn-rimmed spectacles and waving them in the air apolo-
getically. 'The fact is that James MacLean is a very old friend
of mine. We were at Cambridge together and I saw a lot of
him then and afterwards, but our paths diverged, and he tied
himself up in experimental work of rather a dubious nature.
Lost the government a lot of money, and didn't do his own
reputation much good either. I gather that's forgotten, and
he's been reinstated down at Saxmere with his own hand-
picked team of experts and a government grant. They're stuck

for an electronics engineer – which is where you come in. MacLean has sent me an S.O.S. for someone I can vouch for personally – in other words, he wants a chap who won't talk. You'd do me a personal favour if you went.'

Put like this, there was little I could do but accept. It was a damned nuisance, all the same. The last thing in the world I wanted to do was to leave Associated Electronics Ltd, and its unique facilities for research, and drift off to the east coast to work for someone who had blotted his copybook once and might do so again.

'When do you want me to go?' I asked.

The chief looked more apologetic than ever.

'As soon as you can make it. The day after tomorrow? I'm really very sorry, Saunders. With any luck you'll be back by Christmas. I've told MacLean I'm lending you to him for this particular project only. No question of a long-term transfer. You're too valuable here.'

This was the sop. The pat on the back. A.E.L. would forget about me for the next three months. I had another question, though.

'What sort of a chap is he?'

'MacLean?' My chief paused before replacing his horn-rims, always a signal of dismissal. 'He's what I'd call an enthusiast, the kind that don't let go. A fanatic in his way. Oh, he won't bore you. I remember at Cambridge he spent most of his time bird-watching. He had some peculiar theory then about migration, but he didn't inflict it on us. He nearly chucked physics for neurology, but thought better of it – the girl he later married persuaded him. Then came the tragedy. She died after they'd only been married a year.'

My chief replaced his spectacles. He had no more to say or, if he had, it was beside the point. As I was leaving the room he called after me, 'You can keep that last piece of information to yourself. About his wife, I mean. His staff down there may not know anything about it.'

It was not until I had actually packed up at A.E.L. and left my comfortable digs, and the train was drawing out of Liverpool Street station, that the full force of my situation hit me. Here I was, lumbered with a job I didn't want in an outfit I knew nothing about, and all as a personal favour to my chief, who obviously had some private reason for obliging his onetime colleague. As I stared moodily out of the carriage window, feeling more bloody-minded every minute, I kept seeing the expression on my successor's face when I told him I was going to Saxmere.

'That dump?' he said. 'Why, it's a joke – they haven't done any serious research there for years. The Ministry have given it over to the crackpots, hoping they'll blow themselves to pieces.'

A few discreet off-hand inquiries in other quarters had brought the same answer. A friend of mine with a sense of humour advised me over the telephone to take golf-clubs and plenty of paperbacks. 'There's no sort of organisation,' he said. 'MacLean works with a handful of chaps who think he's the Messiah. If you don't fall into line he ignores you, and you'll find yourself doing sweet f.a.'

'Fine. That suits me. I need a holiday,' I lied, hanging up with feelings of intense irritation against the world in general.

It was typical, I suppose, of my approach to the whole business that I hadn't checked thoroughly on timetables, and therefore an added annoyance to find that I had to get out at Ipswich, wait forty minutes, and board a slow train to Thirlwall, which was the station for Saxmere. It was raining when I finally descended upon the empty windswept platform, and the porter who took my ticket told me that the taxi which usually waited for this particular train had been snapped up five minutes before.

'There's a garage opposite the Three Cocks,' he added. 'They might still be open and could run you over to Saxmere.'

I walked past the booking office carrying my bags and blaming myself for my bad staff-work. As I stood outside the station wondering whether to brave the doubtful hospitality of the Three Cocks – it was close on seven, and even if a car was not available I could do with a drink – a very ancient Morris came swerving into the station-yard and pulled up in front of me. The driver got out and made a dive for my bags.

'You are Saunders, I take it?' he asked, smiling. He was young, not more than about nineteen, with a shock of fair hair.

'That's right,' I said. 'I was just wondering where the hell I'd raise a taxi.'

'You wouldn't,' he answered. 'On a wet night the Yanks swipe the lot. Anything on wheels that will take 'em out of Thirlwall. Hop in, will you?'

I'd forgotten about Thirlwall being a U.S. air-base, and made a mental note to avoid the Three Cocks in my leisure hours. American personnel on the loose are not among my favourite companions.

'Sorry about the rattle,' apologised the driver as we swerved through the town to the accompaniment of what sounded like a couple of petrol cans rolling under the back seat. 'I keep meaning to fix it, but never find time. My name's Ryan, by the way, Ken Ryan, always known as Ken. We don't go in for surnames at Saxmere.'

I said nothing. My Christian name is Stephen, nor had anyone ever shortened it to Steve. My gloom increased and I lit a cigarette. Already the houses of Thirlwall lay behind us and our road, having traversed a mile or two of flat countryside consisting of turnip fields, suddenly shot up on to a sandy track across a heath, over which we proceeded in a series of bumps until my head nearly hit the roof.

My companion apologised once more.

'I could have taken you in by the main entrance,' he said, 'but this way is so much shorter. Don't worry, the springs are used to it.'

The sandy track topped a rise and there below us, stretching into infinity, lay acre upon acre of waste land, marsh and reed, bounded on the left by sand-dunes with the open sea beyond. The marshes were intersected here and there by dykes, beside which stood clumps of forlorn rushes bending to the wind and rain, the dykes in their turn forming themselves into dank pools, one or two of them miniature lakes, ringed about with reeds.

Our road, the surface of which was now built up with clinkers and small stones, descended abruptly to this scene of desolation, winding like a narrow ribbon with the marsh on either side. In the far distance a square tower, grey and squat, stood out against the skyline, and as we drew nearer I could see beyond the tower itself the curving spiral of the one-time radar installation, brooding over the waste land like a giant oyster-shell. This, then, was Saxmere. My worst forebodings could not have conjured up a more forbidding place.

My companion, sensing probably from my silence that I lacked enthusiasm, gave me a half-glance.

'It looks a bit grim in this light,' he said, 'but that's the rain. The weather's pretty good on the whole, though the wind is keen. We get some stunning sunsets.'

The laugh with which I greeted his remark was intended to be ironic, but it missed its mark, or was taken as encouragement, for he added, 'If you're keen on birds you've come to the right spot. Avocets breed here in the spring, and last March I heard the bittern boom.'

I choked back the expletive that rose to my lips – his phraseology struck me as naïve – and while admitting indifference to all objects furred or feathered I expressed surprise that anything in such a dreary locality should have a desire to breed at all. My sarcasm was lost, for he said, quite seriously, 'Oh, you'd be surprised,' and ground the Morris to a halt before a gate set in a high wired fence.

'Have to unlock this,' he told me, jumping out of the car, and I saw that now we had come to Saxmere itself. The area ahead was bounded on all sides by this same fence, some ten feet in height, giving the place the look of a concentration camp. This agreeable vista was enhanced by the sudden appearance of an Alsatian dog, who loped out of the marshes to the left, and stood wagging its tail at young Ken as he unlocked the gate.

'Where are the tommy-guns?' I asked, when he climbed back into the driving-seat. 'Or does the dog's handler watch us unseen from some concrete dug-out in the marsh?'

This time he had the grace to laugh as we passed through the barricade. 'No guns, no handlers,' he said. 'Cerberus is as gentle as a lamb. Not that I expected to find him here, but Mac will have him under control.'

He got out once more and locked the gate, while the dog, his head pointing across the marsh, took no more notice of us. Then all at once, pricking his ears, he dived into the reeds, and I watched him running along a narrow muddy track in the direction of the tower.

'He'll be home before we are,' said Ken, letting in the clutch, and the car swerved to the right along a broad asphalt road, the marsh giving place now to scrub and shingle.

The rain had stopped, the clouds had broken into splintered fragments, and the squat tower of Saxmere stood out bold and black against a copper sky. Did this, I wondered, herald one of the famous sunsets? If so, no member of the staff appeared to be taking advantage of it. Road and marsh alike were deserted. We passed the fork to the main entrance and turned left towards the disused radar installation and the tower itself, grouped about with sheds and concrete buildings. The place looked more like a deserted Dachau than ever.

Ken drove past the tower and the main buildings, taking a side road running seaward, at the end of which was a row of prefabricated huts.

'Here we are,' he said, 'and what did I tell you? Cerberus has beaten us to it.'

The dog emerged from a track on the left and ran off behind the huts.

'How is he trained?' I asked. 'A hi-fi whistle?'

'Not exactly,' answered my companion.

I got out of the car and he heaved my bags from the rear seat.

'These are the sleeping-quarters, I suppose?'

I glanced about me. The pre-fabs at least looked wind- and water-tight.

'It's the whole works,' replied Ken. 'We sleep, feed, and do everything here.'

He ignored my stare and led the way ahead. There was a small entrance hall, and a corridor beyond running right and left. Nobody was about. The walls of both hall and corridor were a dull grey, the floor covered with linoleum. The impression was that of a small-town country surgery after hours.

'We feed at eight, but there's loads of time,' said Ken. 'You'd like to see your room and have a bath, perhaps.'

I had no particular desire for a bath, but I badly needed a drink. I followed him down the left-hand corridor, and he opened a door and switched on the light, then crossed the floor and pulled aside the curtains.

'Sorry about that,' he said. 'Janus likes to bed us down early before going through to the kitchen. Winter or summer, these curtains are drawn at six-thirty, and the covers removed from the beds. He's a stickler for routine.'

I looked around. Whoever designed the room must have had a hospital training all right. It had the bare essentials. Bed, wash-basin, chest-of-drawers, wardrobe, one chair. The window gave on to the entrance front. The blankets on the bed were folded hospital fashion, and a military hospital at that.

'O.K.?' asked Ken. He looked puzzled. Possibly my expression surprised him.

'Fine,' I answered. 'Now what about a drink?'

I followed him up the corridor once more, across the entrance hall, and on through a swing-door at the far end. I heard the light clack-clack of ping-pong balls, and braced myself for frivolity. The room we entered was empty. The sportsmen, whoever they were, were playing in the room beyond. Here there were easy chairs, a table or two, an electric fire and a bar in the far corner, behind which my youthful companion installed himself. I noticed, with misgiving, two enormous urns.

'Coffee or cocoa?' he asked. 'Or do you prefer something cool? I can recommend the orange juice with a splash of soda.'

'I'd like a Scotch,' I said.

He looked distressed. His expression became that of an anxious host whose guest demands fresh strawberries in midwinter.

'I'm frightfully sorry,' he said, 'we none of us touch alcohol.

Mac won't have it served, it's one of his things. But of course you can bring your own supply and drink in your room. What a fool I was not to have warned you. We could have stopped at Thirlwall and brought you back a bottle from the Three Cocks.'

His distress was so genuine that I controlled the flood-gates of emotion that threatened to burst from me, and told him I would settle for orange juice. He looked relieved, and splashed the nauseous liquid into a tall glass, deftly sousing it with soda.

I felt the time had come for further explanation, not only about him, the acolyte, but about the rest of the establishment. Was the Order Benedictine or Franciscan, and at what hour would the bell sound for Vespers and Compline?

'Forgive my ignorance,' I said, 'but my briefing before leaving A.E.L. was somewhat short. I don't know the first thing about Saxmere, or what you do here.'

'Oh, don't worry,' he answered, smiling. 'Mac will explain all that.'

He poured some juice into his own glass and said, 'Cheers.' I ignored the toast and listened to the echo of the ping-pong balls.

'You told me,' I continued, 'that all the work was done in this building where we are now.'

'That's right,' he said.

'But where do all the personnel hang out?' I persisted.

'Personnel?' he echoed, frowning. 'There are no personnel. That's to say, there's only Mac, Robbie, Janus – I suppose you'd count Janus – and myself. And now of course you.'

I put down my glass and stared. Was he having me on? No, he seemed perfectly serious. Tossing down his orange juice like a cup-bearer of the gods quaffing ambrosia, he watched me from behind the bar.

'It's O.K., you know,' he said. 'We're a very happy party.'

I did not doubt it. What with cocoa, ping-pong, and the booming bittern, this team of sportsmen would make the members of a Women's Institute seem like trolls.

My baser instincts made me yearn to prick the youngster's pride.

'And what,' I asked, 'is your position on the staff? Ganymede to the professor's Jove?'

To my intense surprise he laughed, and with an ear cocked to the further room, where the sound of balls had ceased, set two more glasses down upon the bar and filled them both with juice.

'How smart of you to guess,' he answered. 'That's roughly the idea . . . to snatch me from this earth to a doubtful heaven. No, seriously, I'm Mac's guinea-pig, along with Janus's daughter and Cerberus the dog.'

At that moment the door opened and two men came into the room.

Instinctively I recognised MacLean. He was fiftyish, craggy, tall, with the pale, rather light blue eyes which I associate with drunkards, criminals and fighter pilots – in my view the three frequently combine. His lightish hair receded from a high forehead, and the prominent nose was matched by a thrusting chin. He wore baggy corduroy trousers and an immense pull-over with a turtle neck.

His companion was sallow, bespectacled and squat. Shorts and a baggy shirt gave him a boy scout appearance, nor did the circular sweat stains under his armpits enhance his charm.

MacLean advanced towards me holding out his hand, the broad smile of welcome suggesting I had already become one of his small band of brothers.

'I'm so very glad to see you,' he said. 'I do hope Ken has been looking after you all right. Such a wretched evening for your first glimpse of Saxmere, but we'll do better for you tomorrow, won't we, Robbie?'

His voice, his manner, was that of an old-fashioned host. I might have been a late arrival at a country-house shoot. He put his hand on my shoulder and urged me towards the bar.

'Orange juice for all, please, Ken,' he said, and, turning to me, 'We've heard tremendous things about you from A.E.L. I can't tell you how grateful I am to them – to John in particular – for allowing you to come. And above all to your-self. We'll do everything we can to make your visit memorable. Robbie, Ken, I want you to drink to – it's Stephen, isn't it? Shall we say Steve? – and to the success of our joint efforts.'

I forced a smile, and felt it become a fixture on my face. Robbie, the boy scout, blinked at me from behind his spectacles.

'Your very good health,' he said. 'I'm the Johannis factotum here. I do everything from exploding gases to taking Ken's temperature, as well as exercising the dog. When in trouble send for me.'

I laughed, then swiftly realised that the falsetto, music-hall comedian voice was in fact his own, and not assumed for the occasion.

We crossed the corridor to a room facing the front, plain and bare like the one we had left, with a table set for four. A long-faced, saturnine fellow, with close-cropped grizzled hair, stood by the sideboard.

'Meet Janus,' Mac said to me. 'I don't know how they feed you at A.E.L., but Janus sees we none of us starve.'

I favoured the steward with a cheerful nod. He replied to it with a grunt, and I instantly doubted his willingness to run errands for me to the Three Cocks. I waited for MacLean to say grace, which would somehow have seemed in character, but none was forthcoming, and Janus set before him an enormous old-fashioned soup tureen shaped like a jerry, from which my new chief ladled a steaming, saffron-coloured brew. It was surprisingly good. The grilled Dover sole that followed was better still, and the cheese soufflé feather-light. The meal took us some fifty minutes to consume, and by the end of it I was ready to make peace with my fellow-men.

Young Ken – whose conversation during dinner had con-sisted of a series of private jokes with Robbie, while MacLean discoursed on mountain climbing in Crete, the beauty of flamingoes on the wing in the Camargue, and the pecu-liar composition of Piero della Francesca's 'Flagellation of

Christ' – was the first to rise from the table and ask leave to be dismissed.

MacLean nodded. 'Don't read too late,' he said. 'Robbie will turn your light out if you do. Nine-thirty's the limit.'

The youngster smiled, and bade the three of us goodnight. I asked whether Ken was in training to race the dog around the marsh and back.

'No,' answered MacLean abruptly, 'but he needs a lot of sleep. Let's to billiards.'

He led the way from the dining-room back to the so-called bar, while I prepared myself for half an hour or so in the room beyond – nothing loath, for I rather fancied myself with a cue – but as we passed through, and I saw nothing but a ping-pong table and a dart-board, Robbie, noticing my puzzled expression, boomed in my ear, 'A quote from Shakespeare, the Serpent of old Nile. Mac means he wants to brief you.' He pushed me gently forward and then vanished. I followed my leader through yet another door, sound-proofed this time, and we entered the chill atmosphere of what appeared to be half-working lab, half-clinic, streamlined and severe. It even had an operating table under a centre light, and instruments and jars behind glass panels on the walls.

'Robbie's department,' said MacLean. 'He can do anything here from developing a virus to taking out your tonsils.'

I made no comment, having small desire to offer myself as a potential victim to the boy scout's doubtful ministrations, and we passed from the laboratory to the room adjoining.

'You'll feel more at home here,' observed MacLean, and as

he switched on the lights I saw that we had reached the electronics department. The first installation to which we came appeared similar to the one we had built for the G.P.O. some years ago – that is to say, a computer capable of speech, though its vocabulary was limited and the actual 'voice' was far from perfect. MacLean's box of tricks, however, had various accessories, and I went up to examine them closely.

'He's neat, don't you think?' said MacLean, rather like a proud father showing off his new-born infant. 'I call him Charon I.'

We all have pet names for our inventions, and Hermes had seemed particularly appropriate for the winged messenger we had developed for the G.P.O. Charon, if I remembered rightly, was the ferryman who conveyed the spirits of the dead across the Styx. I supposed this was MacLean's own brand of humour.

'What does it do?' I asked cautiously.

'It has several functions,' answered MacLean, 'which I'll explain later, but your main concern will be the voice mechanism.'

He went through a starting-up procedure, much as we had done at A.E.L., but the result was very different. The voice reproduction was perfect, and he had got rid of all the hesitation.

'I'm using the computer for certain experiments in the field of hypnosis,' he went on. 'These involve programming it with a series of questions. The answers are then fed back into the computer, and are themselves used to modify the questions that follow. What do you think of that?'

'It's fantastic!' I answered. 'You've gone miles beyond what anybody else is doing.'

I was indeed flabbergasted, and wondered just how he had done it – as well as keeping it all so secret. We thought we had achieved all that could be done in this particular field at A.E.L.

'Yes,' said Mac, 'your experts will hardly improve upon it. Charon 1 will have many uses, especially in the medical world. I won't go into any more details tonight, except to say that it is primarily connected with an experiment I'm working on which the Ministry knows nothing whatever about.'

He smiled, and here we go, I thought, now we're coming to the 'experiments of a dubious nature' which my chief had warned me about. I said nothing, and MacLean moved to a different installation.

'This,' he said, 'is what really concerns the government, and the military chaps in particular. You know, of course, that blast is difficult to control. An aeroplane breaking the sound barrier may shatter windows indiscriminately, but not one particular window, or one particular target. Charon 2 can do just that.' He crossed the room to a cabinet, took out a glass jar, and placed it on the working bench by the wall. Then he threw a switch on his second installation, and the glass shivered to fragments.

'Rather neat, don't you think?' said MacLean. 'But of course the point is the long-range use, should you wish to inflict serious damage on specific objects at a distance. I personally don't – blast doesn't interest me – but the Services would find it effective on occasion. It's just a case of a special method of transmission. But my particular concern is high-frequency

response between individuals, and between people and animals. I'm keeping this quiet from my masters, who give me a
grant.' He put his fingers on another control on the second
installation. 'You won't see anything with this one,' he said.
'It's the call-note with which I control Cerberus. Human
beings can't pick it up.'

We waited in silence, and a few minutes later I heard the
sound of a dog scratching at the further door. MacLean let
him in. 'All right. Good boy. Lie down.' He turned to me,
smiling. 'Nothing really in that – he was only the other side
of the building – but we've got him to obey orders from long
distances. It could be quite useful in an emergency.' He glanced
at his watch. 'I wonder if Mrs J. will forgive me,' he murmured.
'It's only a quarter-past nine after all. And I do so enjoy showing off.' His schoolboy grin was suddenly infectious.

'What are you going to do?' I asked.

'Bring her small daughter to the telephone, or wake her up
if she's asleep.'

He made another adjustment to the apparatus, and once
again we waited. In about two minutes the telephone rang.
MacLean crossed the room to answer it. 'Hullo?' he said.
'Sorry, Mrs J. Just an experiment. I'm sorry if I've woken her
up. Yes, put her on. Hullo, Niki. No, it's all right. You can go
back to bed. Sleep tight.' He replaced the receiver, then bent
down to pat Cerberus stretched at his feet.

'Children, like dogs, are particularly easy to train,' he said.
'Or put it this way – their sixth sense, the one that picks up
these signals, is highly developed. Niki has her own call-note,

just as Cerberus does, and the fact that she suffers from retarded development makes her an excellent subject.'

He patted his box of tricks in much the same fashion that he had patted his dog. Then he glanced up at me and smiled.

'Any questions?'

'Obviously,' I replied. 'The first being, what is the exact object of the exercise? Are you trying to prove that certain high-frequency signals have potentialities not only for destruction but also for controlling the receptive mechanism in an animal, and also the human brain?'

I forced a composure I was far from feeling. If these were the sort of experiments that were going on at Saxmere, small wonder the place had been shrugged aside as a crackpot's paradise.

MacLean looked at me thoughtfully. 'Of course Charon 2 could be said to prove exactly that,' he said, 'though this is not my intention. The Ministry may possibly be very disappointed in consequence. No, I personally am trying to tackle something more far-reaching.' He paused, then put his hand on my shoulder. 'We'll leave Charons 1 and 2 for tonight. Come outside for a breath of air.'

We left by the door which the dog had scratched at. It led to another corridor, and finally to an entrance at the back of the building. MacLean unbolted the door and I followed him through. The rain had ceased and the air was clean and cold, the sky brilliant with stars. In the distance, beyond the line of sand-dunes, I could hear the roar of sea breaking upon shingle.

MacLean inhaled deeply, his face turned seaward. Then he looked upward at the stars. I lit a cigarette and waited for him to speak.

'Have you any experience of poltergeists?' he asked.

'Things that go bump in the night?' I said. 'No, I can't say I have.' I offered him a cigarette, but he shook his head.

'What you watched just now,' said MacLean, 'the glass shivering to pieces, is the same thing. Electrical force, released. Mrs J. had trouble with crashing objects long before I developed Charon. Saucepans, and so on, hurling themselves about at the coastguard's cottage where they live. It was Niki, of course.'

I stared at him, incredulous. 'You mean the child?'

'Yes.'

He thrust his hands in his pockets and began pacing up and down. 'Naturally, she was quite unaware of the fact,' he continued. 'So were her parents. It was only psychic energy exploding, extra strong in her case because her brain is undeveloped, and since she is the only survivor of identical twins the force was doubled.'

This was rather too much to swallow, and I laughed. He swung round and faced me.

'Have you a better solution?' he asked.

'No,' I admitted, 'but surely . . .'

'Exactly,' he interrupted. 'Nobody ever has. There are hundreds, thousands of cases of these so-called phenomena, and almost every time they are reported there is evidence to show that a child, or someone who is regarded as of sub-standard intelligence, was in the locality at the time.' He resumed his walk and I beside him, the dog at our heels.

'So what?' I said.

'So that,' he went on, 'it suggests we all possess an untapped source of energy within us that awaits release. Call it, if you like, Force Six. It works in the same way as the high-frequency impulse which I released just now from Charon. Here is the explanation of telepathy, precognition, and all the so-called psychic mysteries. The power we develop in any electronic device is the same as the power that the Janus child possesses – with one difference, to date: we can control the one but not the other.'

I saw his meaning, but not where the discussion was leading us. God knows life is complicated enough without seeking to probe the unconscious forces that may lie dormant within man, especially if the connecting link must first be an animal, or an idiot child.

'All right,' I said, 'so you tap this Force Six, as you call it. Not only in Janus's daughter, but in all animals, in backward children, and finally in the human race. You have us breaking glasses, sending saucepans flying, exchanging messages by telepathic communication, and so on and so forth; but wouldn't it add immeasurably to our difficulties, so that we ended up in the complete chaos from which we presumably sprang?'

This time it was MacLean who laughed. Our walk had taken us to a ridge of high ground, and we were looking across the sand-dunes to the sea beyond. The long shingle beach seemed to stretch into eternity, as drear and featureless as the marsh behind it. The sea broke with a monotonous roar, sucking at the dragging stones, only to renew the effort and spend itself once more.

'No doubt it would,' he said, 'but that's not what I'm after. Man will find a proper use for Force Six in his own good time. I want to make it work for him after the body dies.'

I threw my cigarette on to the ground and watched it glow an instant before it flickered to a wet stub.

'What on earth do you mean?' I asked him.

He was looking at me, trying to size up my reaction to his words. I could not make up my mind if he was mad or not, but there was something vaguely endearing about him as he stood there, hunched, speculative, like an overgrown schoolboy in his corduroy bags and his old turtle-necked sweater.

'I'm quite serious,' he said. 'The energy is there, you know, when it leaves the body on the point of death. Think of the appalling wastage through the centuries; all that energy escaping as we die, when it might be used for the benefit of mankind. It's the oldest of theories, of course, that the soul escapes through the nostrils or the mouth – the Greeks believed in it, so do certain African tribes today. You and I are not concerned with souls, and we know that our intelligence dies with our body. But not the vital spark. The life-force continues as energy, uncontrolled, and up to the present . . . useless. It's above us and around us as we stand talking here.'

Once again he threw back his head and looked at the stars, and I wondered what deep inner loneliness had driven him to this vain quest after the intangible. Then I remembered that his wife had died. Doubtless this theoretical bunk had saved him.

'I'm afraid it will take you a lifetime to prove,' I said to him.

'No,' he answered. 'At the most a couple of months. You see, Charon 3, which I didn't show you, has a built-in storage unit, to receive and contain power, or, to be exact, to receive and contain Force Six when it is available.' He paused. The glance he threw at me was curious, speculative. I waited for him to continue. 'The ground work has all been done,' he said. 'We are geared and ready for the great experiment, when Charons 1 and 3 will be used in conjunction, but I need an assistant, fully trained to work both installations, when the moment comes. I'll be perfectly frank with you. Your predecessor here at Saxmere wouldn't co-operate. Oh yes, you had one. I asked your chief at A.E.L. not to tell you – I preferred to tell you myself. Your predecessor refused his co-operation for reasons of conscience which I respect.'

I stared. I was not surprised at the other fellow refusing to co-operate, but I did not see where ethics came into it.

'He was a Catholic,' explained MacLean. 'Believing as he did in the survival of the soul and its sojourn in purgatory, he couldn't stomach any idea of imprisoning the life force and making it work for us here on earth. Which, as I have told you, is my intention.'

He turned away from the sea and began walking back the way we had come. The lights were all extinguished in the low line of pre-fabs where presumably we were to eat, work, sleep and have our being during the eight weeks that lay ahead. Behind them loomed the square tower of the disused radar station, a monument to the ingenuity of man.

'They told me at A.E.L. you had no religious scruples,' went on MacLean. 'Neither have the rest of us at Saxmere, though we like to think of ourselves as dedicated men. As young Ken puts it himself, it comes to the same thing as giving your eyes to a hospital, or your kidneys to cold storage. The problem is ours, not his.'

I had a sudden recollection of the youngster at the bar, pouring out the orange juice and calling himself a guinea-pig.

'What's Ken's part in all this, then?' I asked.

MacLean paused in his walk and looked straight at me.

'The boy has leukaemia,' he said. 'Robbie gives him three months at the outside. There'll be no pain. He has tremendous guts, and believes wholeheartedly in the experiment. It's very possible the attempt may fail. If it fails, we lose nothing – his life is forfeit anyway. If we succeed . . .' He broke off, catching his breath as though swept by a sudden deep emotion. 'If we succeed, you see what it will mean?' he said. 'We shall have the answer at last to the intolerable futility of death.'

When I awoke next morning to a brilliant day and looked from my bedroom window along the asphalt road to the disused radar tower, brooding like a sentinel over empty sheds and rusted metal towards the marsh beyond, I made my decision then and there to go.

I shaved, bathed, and went along to breakfast determined

to be courteous to all, and to ask for five minutes alone with MacLean immediately afterwards. I would catch the first available train, and with luck be in London by one o'clock. If there was any unpleasantness with A.E.L. my chief would take the rap for it, not I.

The dining-room was empty except for Robbie, who was attacking an enormous plateful of soused herrings. I bade him a brief good day and helped myself to bacon. I looked round for a morning paper but there was none. Conversation would be forced upon me.

'Fine morning,' I observed.

He did not answer me immediately. He was engaged in dissecting his herring with the finesse of an expert. Then his falsetto voice came at me across the table.

'Are you proposing to back out?' he asked.

His question took me by surprise, and I disliked the note of derision.

'I'm an electronics engineer,' I answered, 'I'm not interested in psychical research.'

'No more were Lister's colleagues concerned with discovering antisepsis,' he rejoined. 'What fools they were made to look later.'

He forked a half-herring into his mouth and proceeded to chew it, watching me from behind his bi-focal specs.

'So you believe all this stuff about Force Six?' I said.

'Don't you?' he parried.

I pushed aside my plate in protest.

'Look here,' I said. 'I can accept this work MacLean has

done on sound. He has found the answer to voice production which we failed to do at A.E.L. He has developed a system by which high-frequency waves can be picked up by animals, and also, it seems, by one idiot child. I give him full marks for the first, am doubtful about the potential value of the second, and as to his third project – capturing the life-force, or whatever he calls it, as it leaves the body – if anyone talked to the Ministry about that one, your boss would find himself inside.'

I resumed my bacon feeling I had put Robbie in his place. He finished his herrings, then started on the toast and marmalade.

'Ever watched anyone die?' he asked suddenly.

'As a matter of fact, no,' I answered.

'I'm a doctor, and it's part of my job,' he said, 'in hospitals, in homes, in refugee camps after the war. I suppose I've witnessed scores of deaths during my professional life. It's not a pleasant experience. Here at Saxmere it's become my business to stand by a very plucky, likeable lad, not only during his last hours, but during the few weeks that remain to him. I could do with some help.'

I got up and took my plate to the sideboard. Then I returned and helped myself to coffee.

'I'm sorry,' I said.

He pushed the toast-rack towards me but I shook my head. Breakfast is not my favourite meal, and this morning I lacked appetite. There was a sound of footsteps outside on the asphalt, and a head looked in at the window. It was Ken.

'Hullo,' he said, with a grin, 'what a wonderful morning.

If Mac doesn't need you in the control room I'll show you round. We could take a walk up to the coastguard cottages and over Saxmere cliff. Are you game?' He took my hesitation for assent. 'Splendid! It's no use asking Robbie. He'll spend the morning in the lab gloating over specimens of my blood.'

The head vanished, and I heard him call to Janus through the kitchen window alongside. Neither Robbie nor I spoke. The sound of munching toast became unbearable. I stood up.

'Where will I find MacLean?' I asked.

'In the control room,' he answered, and went on eating.

It was best done at once. I went the way I had been shown the night before, through the swing door to the lab. Somehow the operating table under the centre light held more significance this morning, and I avoided looking at it. I went through the door at the far end, and saw MacLean standing by Charon 1. He beckoned me over.

'There's a slight fault in the processing unit,' he said. 'I noticed it last night. I'm sure you'll be able to fix it.'

This was the moment to express my regrets and tell him I had decided against joining his team and intended to return to London immediately. I did no such thing. Instead I crossed the floor to the computer and stood by while he explained the circuits. Professional pride, professional jealousy, if you will, coupled with intense curiosity to know why this particular apparatus was superior to the one we had built at A.E.L., proved too much for me.

'There are some overalls on the wall,' said MacLean. 'Put 'em on, and we'll fix the fault between us.'

From then onward I was lost, or perhaps it would be more correct to say that I was won. Not to his lunatic theories, not to any future experiment with life and death; I was conquered by the supreme beauty and efficiency of Charon 1 itself. Beauty, may be an odd word to use where electronics are concerned. I did not find it so. Herein lay all my passion, all my feelings; from my boyhood I had been involved with the creation of these things. This was my life's work. I was not interested in the uses to which the machines I had helped to develop and perfect were ultimately put. My part was to see that they fulfilled the function for which they were designed. Until arriving at Saxmere I had had no other object, no other aim in life, but to do what I was fitted to do, and do it well.

Charon 1 awakened something else in me, an awareness of power. I had only to handle those controls to know that what I wanted now was to have detailed knowledge of all the working parts, and then be given charge of the whole lay-out. Nothing else mattered. By the end of that first morning I had not only located the fault, a minor one, but had set it right. MacLean had become Mac, the shortening of my name to Steve was something that no longer jarred, and the whole fantastic set-up had ceased to irritate or to dismay; I had become one of the team.

Robbie showed no surprise when I turned up at lunch-time, nor did he allude to our conversation at breakfast. In the late afternoon, with Mac's permission, I took my suggested walk with Ken. It was impossible to connect approaching death with this irrepressible youngster, and I put it from my mind.

It could be that both Mac and Robbie were wrong about it. Anyway, it was not, thank God, my problem.

He showed no sign of fatigue and led the way, laughing and chatting, across the sand-dunes to the sea. The sun was shining, the air felt cold and clean, even the long stretch of shore that had seemed dreary the night before had now a latent charm. The heavy shingle gave place to sand, crisp under our feet; Cerberus, who accompanied us, bounded ahead. We threw sticks for him to retrieve from the pallid, almost effortless, sea, which gently, without menace, broke beside us as we walked. We did not discuss Saxmere, or anything connected with it; instead Ken regaled me with amusing gossip about the U.S. base at Thirlwall, where he had apparently worked as one of the ground staff before Mac arranged his transfer ten months before.

Suddenly Cerberus, barking puppy-fashion for another stick, turned and stood motionless, ears pricked, head to wind. Then he started loping back the way we had come, his lithe black-and-tan form soon lost to sight against the darker shingle and the dunes beyond.

'He's had a signal from Charon,' said Ken.

The night before, watching Mac at the controls, the dog's scratching at the door seemed natural. Here, some three miles distant on the lonely shore, his swift departure was uncanny.

'Effective, isn't it?' said Ken.

I nodded; but somehow, because of what I'd seen, my spirits left me. Enthusiasm for the walk had waned. It would have been different had I been alone. Now, with the boy beside me,

I was, as it were, confronted with the future, the project Mac had in mind, the months ahead.

'Want to turn back?' he asked me.

His words reminded me of Robbie's at breakfast, though he meant them otherwise. 'Just as you like,' I said indifferently.

He swung left and we clambered, slipping and sliding with every step, up the steep slope to the cliffs above the beach. I was breathless when I reached the top. Not Ken. Smiling, he lent a hand to pull me up. Heather and scrub lay all about us, and the wind was in our faces, stronger than it had been below. About a quarter of a mile distant, stark and white against the skyline, stood a row of coastguard cottages, bleak windows all aflame with the setting sun.

'Come and pay your respects to Mrs J.,' suggested Ken.

Reluctantly I followed, detesting unpremeditated visits, no matter where. The unprepossessing Janus household did not attract me. As he drew near I saw that only the far cottage was inhabited. The others had the forlorn, lost look of buildings untenanted for years. Two had their windows broken. Gardens, untended, sprawled. Posts, sagging drunkenly from the damp earth, trailed pieces of barbed wire from their rotting stumps. A small girl was leaning over the gate of the occupied cottage. Dark, straight hair framed her pinched face, her eyes were lustreless, and she was wanting a front tooth.

'Hullo, Niki,' called Ken.

The child stared, then slowly removed herself from the gate. Morosely, she pointed at me. 'Who's that?' she asked.

'His name is Steve,' Ken answered her.

'I don't like his shoes,' said the child.

Ken laughed and opened the gate, and as he did so the child attempted to climb upon him. Gently he put her aside, and walking up the path to the open door called, 'Are you there, Mrs J.?'

A woman appeared, pallid and dark like her child. Her anxious face broke into a smile at the sight of Ken. She bade us enter, apologising for the disarray. I was introduced as Steve, and we hovered uncomfortably in the front room, where the child's toys were strewn about the floor.

'We've had tea,' Ken said, in reply to Mrs J.'s question, but, insisting that the kettle had just boiled, the woman vanished to the adjoining kitchen, to reappear at once with a large brown tea-pot and two cups and saucers. There was nothing for it but to swallow the stuff under her watchful eyes, while the child, edging against Ken all the while, stared balefully at my inoffensive canvas shoes.

I gave full marks to my young companion. He exchanged pleasantries with Mrs Janus, and patted the unendearing Niki. I remained silent throughout, and wondered why the child's likeness, framed in place of honour over the fireplace, should be so much more pleasing than the child herself.

'It's very cold here in the winter, but a bracing cold,' said Mrs Janus, fixing me with her own mournful eyes. 'I always say I prefer the frost to the damp.'

I agreed and shook my head at the offer of more tea. At this moment the child stiffened. She stood rigid a moment, her eyes closed. I wondered if she were going to throw a fit. Then very calmly she announced, 'Mac wants me.'

Mrs Janus, with a murmur of apology, went into the hall and I heard her dial. Ken was watching the child, himself unmoved. I felt slightly sick. In a moment I heard Mrs Janus speaking over the telephone and she called, 'Niki, come here and speak to Mac.'

The child ran from the room, and for the first time since our arrival showed animation. She even laughed. Mrs Janus returned and smiled at Ken.

'I think Mac really wants a word with you,' she said.

Ken got up and went into the hall. Alone with the child's mother, I did not know what to say. At last, in desperation, nodding at the photograph above the fireplace, I said, 'What a good likeness of Niki. Taken a few years ago, I suppose?'

To my dismay, the woman's eyes filled with tears.

'That's not Niki, that's her twin,' she answered. 'That's our Penny. We lost her soon after they had both turned five.'

My awkward apology was cut short by the entrance of the child herself. Ignoring my shoes she came straight to me, put her hand on my knee and announced, 'Mac says Cerberus is back. And you and Ken can go home.'

'Thank you,' I said.

As we walked away from the cottages, over scrub and heather, and took a short cut back to Saxmere through the marsh, I asked Ken whether the call-signal from Charon invariably had the effect I had seen, that of awakening latent intelligence in the child.

'Yes,' he said. 'We don't know why. Robbie thinks the ultra-short-wave may have therapeutic value in itself. Mac doesn't agree. He believes that when he puts out the call it connects Niki with what he calls Force Six, which in her case is doubled because of the dead twin.'

Ken spoke as if this fantastic theory was perfectly natural.

'Do you mean,' I asked, 'that when the call goes through the dead twin somehow takes over?'

Ken laughed. He walked so fast it was hard to keep up with him.

'Ghoulies and ghosties?' he queried. 'Good Lord, no! There's nothing left of poor Penny but electric energy, still attached to her living twin. That's why Niki makes such a useful guinea-pig.'

He glanced across at me, smiling.

'When I go,' he said, 'Mac plans to tap my energy too. Don't ask me how. I just don't know. But he's welcome to have a crack at it.'

We went on walking. The sour smell of stagnant water rose from the marsh on either side of us. The wind strengthened, flattening the reeds. The tower of Saxmere loomed ahead, hard and black against a russet sky.

I had the voice production unit functioning to my satisfaction within the next few days. We fed it with tape, programmed in advance as we had done at A.E.L., but the vocabulary was more extensive, consisting of a call signal 'This is Charon speaking . . . this is Charon speaking . . .' followed by a series of numbers, spoken with great clarity. Then came questions, most of them quite simple, such as, 'Are you O.K.?' 'Does anything bother you?', proceeding to statements of fact like, 'You are not with us. You are at Thirlwall. It is two years back. Tell us what you see,' and so on. My job was to control the precision of the voice, the programme was Mac's responsibility, and, if the questions and statements appeared inane to me, doubtless they made sound sense to him.

On Friday he told me that he considered Charon was ready for use the next day, and Robbie and Ken were warned for eleven a.m. Mac himself would be at the controls, and I was to watch. In the light of what I had already witnessed, I should have been fully prepared for what happened. Oddly enough, I was not. I took up my station in the adjoining lab, while Ken stretched himself out on the operating-table.

'It's all right,' he said to me with a wink. 'Robbie isn't going to carve me up.'

There was a microphone in position above his head, with a lead going through to Charon 1. A yellow light for 'Stand-by' flashed on the wall. It changed to red. I saw Ken close his eyes. Then a voice came from Charon. 'This is Charon speaking . . . This is Charon speaking.' The series of numbers followed, and, after a pause, the question, 'Are you O.K.?'

When Ken replied, 'Yes, I'm O.K.' I noticed that his voice lacked its usual buoyancy; it was flatter, pitched in a lower key. I glanced at Robbie; he handed me a slip of paper on which were written the words, 'He's under hypnosis'.

The penny dropped, and I realised for the first time the full

33

importance of the sound unit and the reason for perfecting it. Ken had been conditioned to hypnosis by the electronic voice. The questions on the programme were not haphazard, they were taped for him. The implications of this were even more shocking to me than when I had seen the dog and the child obey the call signal from a distance. When Ken, jokingly, had spoken of 'going to work', this was what he had meant.

'Does anything bother you?' asked the voice.

There was a long pause before the answer, and when it came the tone was impatient, almost fretful.

'It's the hanging about. I want it to happen quickly. If it could be over and done with, then I wouldn't give a damn.'

I might have been standing by a confessional, and I understood now why my predecessor had turned in his job. I saw Robbie's eyes upon me; the demonstration had been staged not only to show Ken's co-operation under hypnosis, proved no doubt dozens of times already, but to test my nerve. The ordeal continued. Much of what Ken said made painful hearing. I don't want to repeat it here. It revealed the unconscious strain under which he lived, never outwardly apparent either to us or to himself.

The programme Mac used was not one I had heard before, and it ended with the words, 'You'll be all right, Ken. You aren't alone. We're with you every step of the way. O.K.?'

A faint smile passed over the quiet face.

'O.K.'

Then the numbers were repeated, in swifter sequence, ending with the words 'Wake up, Ken!'

The boy stretched himself, opened his eyes and sat up. He looked first at Robbie, then at me, and grinned.

'Did old Charon do his stuff?' he asked.

'One hundred per cent,' I answered, my voice falsely hearty.

Ken slid off the operating table, his work for the morning done. I went through to Mac, standing by the controls.

'Thanks, Steve,' he said. 'You can appreciate the necessity for Charon 1 now. An electronic voice, plus a planned programme, eliminates emotion on our part, which will be essential when the time comes. That's the reason Ken has been conditioned to the machine. He responds very well. But better, of course, if the child is with him.'

'The child?' I repeated.

'Yes,' he answered. 'Niki is an essential part of the experiment. She is conditioned to the voice too, and the pair of them chat away together as gay as crickets. They know nothing about it afterwards, naturally.' He paused, watching me closely as Robbie had done. 'Ken will almost certainly go into coma at the end. The child will be our only link with him then. Now, I suggest you borrow a car, drive into Thirlwall and buy yourself a drink.'

He turned away, craggy, imperturbable, suggesting a benevolent bird of prey.

I didn't go into Thirlwall. I walked out across the sand-dunes to the sea. There was nothing calm about it today. Turbulent and grey, it sank into troughs before breaking on the shingle with a roar. Miles away along the beach a group of U.S. Air Corps cadets were practising bugle calls. The shrill notes, the discordant sounds, drove towards me down the wind. For no reason at all the half-forgotten lines of a Negro spiritual kept repeating themselves over and over in my mind.

'He has the whole world in his hands,
He has the whole world in his hands . . .'

The demonstration was repeated, with varying programmes, every three days during the weeks that followed. Mac and I took it in turn at the controls. I soon grew accustomed to this, and the bizarre sessions became a matter of routine.

It was, as Mac had said, less painful when the child was present. Her father would bring her to the lab and leave her with us, Ken already in position and under control. The child would sit in a chair beside him, also with a microphone above her head to record her speech. She was told that Ken was asleep. Then, in her turn, she would receive the signal from Charon, and a different series of numbers from Ken's, after which she would be under control. The programme was different when the two were working together. Charon would take Ken back in time, to a period when he was the same age as Niki, saying, 'You are seven years old. Niki has come to play with you. She is your friend,' and a similar message would be given to the child, 'Ken has come to play with you. He is a boy of your age.'

The two would then chat together, without interruption from Charon, with the quite fantastic result – this had been built up during the past months, I gathered – that the pair were now close friends 'in time', hiding nothing from each other, playing imaginary games, exchanging ideas. Niki, backward and morose when conscious, was lively and gay under control. The taped conversations were checked after each session, to record the increasingly closer rapport between the two, and to act as guide for further programmes. Ken, when conscious, looked upon Niki as Janus's backward child, a sad little object of no interest. He was totally ignorant of what happened when under control. I was not so sure about Niki. Intuition seemed to draw her to him. She would hang about him, if given the chance.

I asked Robbie what the Janus parents felt about the sessions.

'They'd do anything for Mac,' he told me, 'and they believe it may help Niki. The other twin was normal, you see.'

'Do they realise about Ken?'

'That he's going to die?' replied Robbie. 'They've been told, but I doubt if they understand. Who would, looking at him now?'

We were at the bar, and from where we stood we could see Ken and Mac engaged in a game of ping-pong in the room beyond.

Early in December we had a scare. A letter came from the Ministry asking how the Saxmere experiments were going, and could they send someone down to have a look round? We had a consultation, the upshot of which was that I undertook to go up to London to choke them off. By this time I was wholeheartedly behind Mac in all he was doing, and during my brief stay in town I succeeded in satisfying the authorities in question that a visit at this moment would be premature, but we hoped to have something to show them before Christmas. Their interest, of course, lay in Charon 2's potentialities for blast; they knew nothing of Mac's intended project.

When I returned, alighting at Saxmere station in a very different mood from that of three months past, the Morris was waiting for me, but without Ken's cheerful face at the wheel. Janus had replaced him. He was never a talkative bloke, and he answered my question with a shrug.

'Ken's got a cold,' he said. 'Robbie's keeping him in bed as a precaution.'

I went straight to the boy's room on arrival. He looked a bit flushed, but was in his usual spirits, full of protests against Robbie.

'There's absolutely nothing the matter,' he said. 'I got wet feet stalking a bird down in the marsh.'

I sat with him awhile, joking about London and the Ministry, then went to report to Mac.

'Ken has some fever,' he said at once. 'Robbie's done a blood test. It's not too good.' He paused. 'This could be it.'

I felt suddenly chilled. After a moment I told him about London. He nodded briefly.

'Whatever happens,' he said, 'we can't have them here now.'

I found Robbie in the lab, busy with slides and a microscope. He was preoccupied, and hadn't much time for me.

'It's too soon to say yet,' he said. 'Another forty-eight hours should show one way or the other. There's an infection in the right lung. With leukaemia that could be fatal. Go and keep Ken amused.'

I took a portable gramophone along to the boy's bedroom. I suppose I put on about a dozen records, and he seemed quite cheerful. Later he dozed off and I sat there, wondering what to do. My mouth felt dry, and I kept swallowing. Something inside me kept saying, 'Don't let it happen.'

Conversation at dinner was forced. Mac talked about under-graduate days at Cambridge, while Robbie reminisced over past Rugby games – he'd played scrum-half for Guy's. I don't think I talked at all. I went along afterwards to say goodnight to Ken, but he was already asleep. Janus was sitting with him. Back in my room I flung myself on my bed and tried to read, but I couldn't concentrate. There was fog at sea, and every few minutes the fog-horn boomed from the lighthouse along the coast. There was no other sound.

Next morning Mac came to my room at a quarter to eight.

'Ken's worse,' he said. 'Robbie's going to try a blood trans-fusion. Janus will assist.' Janus was a trained orderly.

'What do you want me to do?' I asked.

'Help me get Charons 1 and 3 ready for action,' he said. 'If Ken doesn't respond, I may decide to put phase one of Operation Styx into effect. Mrs J. has been warned we may need the child.'

As I finished dressing I kept telling myself that this was the moment we had been training for all through the past two and a half months. It didn't help. I swallowed some coffee and went to the control room. The door to the lab was closed. They had Ken in there, giving him the blood transfusion. Mac

and I worked over both Charons, seeing that everything functioned perfectly, and that there could be no hitch when the
time came. Programmes, tapes, microphones, all were ready.
After that it was a matter of standing by until Robbie came
through with his report. We got it at about half-past twelve.

'Slight improvement.' They had taken him back to his
room. We all had something to eat while Janus continued his
watch over Ken. Today there was no question of forced conversation. The work on hand was the concern of all. I felt
calmer, steadier. The morning's work had knocked me into
shape. Mac proposed a game of ping-pong after lunch, and
whereas the night before I would have felt aghast at the sug-
gestion, today it seemed the right thing to do. Looking from
the window, between games, I saw Niki wandering up and
down with Mrs Janus, a strange, lost-looking little figure, filling
a battered doll's pram with sticks and stones. She had been on
the premises since ten o'clock.

At half-past four Robbie came into the sports room. I could
tell by his face that it was no good. He shook his head when
Mac suggested another transfusion. It would be a waste of
time, he told us.

'He's conscious?' asked Mac.

'Yes,' answered Robbie. 'I'll bring him through when you're
ready.'

Mac and I went back to the control room. Phase two of
Operation Styx consisted of bringing the operating table in
here, placing it between the three Charons, and connecting up

with an oxygen unit alongside. The microphones were already in position. We had done the manoeuvre often before, in practice runs, but today we beat our fastest time by two minutes.

'Good work,' said Mac.

The thought struck me that he had been looking forward to this moment for months, perhaps for years. He pressed the button to signal that we were ready, and in less than four minutes Robbie and Janus arrived with Ken on the trolley, and lifted him on to the table. I hardly recognised him. The eyes, usually so luminous, had almost disappeared into the sunken face. He looked bewildered. Mac quickly attached electrodes, one against each temple and others to his chest and neck, connecting him to Charon 3. Then he bent over the boy.

'It's all right,' he said. 'We've got you in the lab to do a few tests. Just relax, and you'll be fine.'

Ken stared up at Mac, and then he smiled. We all knew that this was the last we should see of his conscious self. It was, in fact, goodbye. Mac looked at me, and I put Charon 1 into operation, the voice ringing clear and true. 'This is Charon calling . . . This is Charon calling . . .' Ken closed his eyes. He was under hypnosis. Robbie stood beside him, finger on pulse. I set the programme in motion. We had numbered it X in the files, because it was different from the others.

'How do you feel, Ken?'

Even with the microphone close to his lips we could barely hear the answer. 'You know damn well how I feel.'

'Where are you, Ken?'

'I'm in the control room. Robbie's turned the heating off. I've got the idea now. It's to freeze me, like butcher's meat. Ask Robbie to bring back the heat . . .' There was a long pause, and then he said, 'I'm standing by a tunnel. It looks like a tunnel. It could be the wrong end of a telescope, the figures look so small . . . Tell Robbie to bring back the heat.'

Mac, who was beside me at the controls, made an adjustment, and we let the programme run without sound until it reached a certain point, when it was amplified once more to reach Ken.

'You are five years old, Ken. Tell us how you feel.'

There was a long pause and then, to my dismay, though I suppose I should have been prepared for it, Ken whimpered, 'I don't feel well. I don't want to play.'

Mac pressed a button, and the door at the far end opened. Janus pushed his daughter into the room, then closed the door again. Mac had her under control with her call-sign at once, and she did not see Ken on the table. She went and sat down in her chair and closed her eyes.

'Tell Ken you are here, Niki.'

I saw the child clutch the arms of her chair.

'Ken's sick,' she said. 'He's crying. He doesn't want to play.'

The voice of Charon went ruthlessly on.

'Make Ken talk, Niki.'

'Ken won't talk,' said the child. 'He's going to say his prayers.'

Ken's voice came faintly through the microphone to the loudspeakers. The words were gabbled, indistinct.

'Gen'ral Jesus, mekan mild,
Look'pon little child,
Pity my simple city,
Sofa me to come to thee . . .'

There was a long pause after this. Neither Ken nor Niki said anything. I kept my hands on the controls, ready to continue the programme when Mac nodded. Niki began drumming her feet on the floor. All at once she said, 'I shan't go down the tunnel after Ken. It's too dark.'

Robbie, watching his patient, looked up. 'He's gone into coma,' he said.

Mac signalled to me to set Charon 1 in motion again.

'Go after Ken, Niki,' said the voice.

The child protested. 'It's black in there,' she said. She was nearly crying. She hunched herself in her chair and went through crawling motions. 'I don't want to go,' she said. 'It's too long, and Ken won't wait for me.'

She started to tremble all over. I looked across at Mac. He questioned Robbie with a glance.

'He won't come out of it,' Robbie said. 'It may last hours.'

Mac ordered the oxygen apparatus to be put into operation, and Robbie fixed the mask on Ken. Mac went over to Charon 3 and switched on the monitor display screen. He made some adjustments and nodded at me. 'I'll take over,' he said.

The child was still crying, but the next command from Charon 1 gave her no respite. 'Stay with Ken,' it said. 'Tell us what happens.'

I hoped Mac knew what he was doing. Suppose the child went into a coma too? Could he bring her back? Hunched in her chair, she was as still as Ken, and about as lifeless. Robbie told me to put blankets round her and feel her pulse. It was faint, but steady. Nothing happened for over an hour. We watched the flickering and erratic signals on the screen, as the electrodes transmitted Ken's weakening brain impulses. Still the child did not speak.

Later, much later, she stirred, then moved with a strange twisting motion. She crossed her arms over her breast, humping her knees. Her head dropped forward. I wondered if, like Ken, she was engaged in some childish prayer. Then I realised that her position was that of a foetus before birth. Personality had vanished from her face. She looked wizened, old.

Robbie said, 'He's going.'

Mac beckoned me to the controls, and Robbie bent over Ken with fingers on his pulse. The signals on the screen were fainter, and faltering, but suddenly they surged in a strong upward beat, and in the same instant Robbie said, 'It's all over. He's dead.'

The signal was rising and falling steadily now. Mac disconnected the electrodes and turned back to watch the screen. There was no break in the rhythm of the signal, as it moved up and down, up and down, like a heartbeat, like a pulse.

'We've done it!' said Mac. 'Oh, my God . . . we've done it!'

We stood there, the three of us, watching the signal that never for one instant changed its pattern. It seemed to contain, in its confident movement, the whole of life.

I don't know how long we stayed there – it could have been minutes, hours. At last Robbie said, 'What about the child?'

We had forgotten Niki, just as we had forgotten the quiet, peaceful body that had been Ken. She was still lying in her strange, cramped position, her head bowed to her knees. I went to the controls of Charon 1 to operate the voice, but Mac waved me aside.

'Before we wake her, we'll see what she has to say,' he said.

He put through the call signal very faintly, so as not to shock her to consciousness too soon. I followed with the voice, which repeated the final programme command.

'Stay with Ken. Tell us what happens.'

At first there was no response. Then slowly she uncoiled, her gestures odd, uncouth. Her arms fell to her side. She began to rock backwards and forwards as though following the motion on the screen. When she spoke her voice was sharp, pitched high.

'He wants you to let him go,' she said, 'that's what he wants. Let go . . . let go . . . let go . . .' Still rocking she began to gasp for breath, and, lifting her arms, pummelled the air with her fists.

'Let go . . . let go . . . let go . . . let go . . .'

Robbie said urgently, 'Mac, you've got to wake her.'

On the screen the rhythm of the signal had quickened. The child began to choke. Without waiting for Mac, I set the voice in motion.

'This is Charon speaking . . . This is Charon speaking . . . Wake up, Niki.'

The child shuddered, and the suffused colour drained from her face. Her breathing became normal. She opened her eyes. She stared at each of us in turn in her usual apathetic way, and proceeded to pick her nose.

'I want to go to the toilet,' she said sullenly.

Robbie led her from the room. The signal, which had increased its speed during the child's outburst, resumed its steady rise and fall.

'Why did it alter speed?' I asked.

'If you hadn't panicked and woken her up, we might have found out,' Mac said.

His voice was harsh, quite unlike himself.

'Mac,' I protested, 'that kid was choking to death.'

'No,' he said, 'no, I don't think so.'

He turned and faced me. 'Her movements simulated the shock of birth,' he said. 'Her gasp for air was the first breath of an infant, struggling for life. Ken, in coma, had gone back to that moment, and Niki was with him.'

I knew by this time that almost anything was possible under hypnosis, but I wasn't convinced.

'Mac,' I said, 'Niki's struggle came *after* Ken was dead, *after* the new signal appeared on Charon 3. Ken couldn't have gone back to the moment of birth – he was already dead, don't you see?'

He did not answer at once. 'I just don't know,' he said at last. 'I think we shall have to put her under control again.'

'No,' said Robbie. He had entered the lab while we were talking. 'That child has had enough. I've sent her home, and told her mother to put her to bed.'

I had never heard him speak with authority before. He looked away from the lighted screen back to the still body on the table. 'Doesn't that go for the rest of us?' he said. 'Haven't we all had enough? You've proved your point, Mac. I'll celebrate with you tomorrow, but not tonight.'

He was ready to break. So, I think, were we all. We had barely eaten through the day, and when Janus returned he set about getting us a meal. He had taken the news of Ken's death with his usual calm. The child, he told us, had fallen asleep the moment she was put to bed.

So . . . it was all over. Reaction, exhaustion, numbness of feeling, all three set in, and I yearned, like Niki, for the total release of sleep.

Before dragging myself to bed some impulse, stronger than the aching fatigue that overwhelmed me, urged me back to the control room. Everything was as we had left it. Ken's body lay on the table, covered with a blanket. The screen was lighted still, and the signal was pulsing steadily up and down. I waited a moment, then I bent to the tape-control, setting it to play back that last outburst from the child. I remembered the rocking head, the hands fighting to be free, and switched it on.

'He wants you to let him go,' said the high-pitched voice, 'that's what he wants. Let go . . . let go . . . let go . . .' Then came the gasp for breath, and the words were repeated. 'Let go . . . let go . . . let go . . . let go . . .'

I switched it off. The words did not make sense. The signal was simply electrical energy, trapped at the actual moment

47

of Ken's death. How could the child have translated this into a cry for freedom, unless . . . ?

I looked up. Mac was watching me from the doorway. The dog was with him.

'Cerberus is restless,' he said. 'He keeps padding backwards and forwards in my room. He won't let me sleep.'

'Mac,' I said, 'I've played that recording again. There's something wrong.'

He came and stood beside me. 'What do you mean, something wrong? The recording doesn't affect the issue. Look at the screen. The signal's steady. The experiment has been a hundred per cent successful. We've done what we set out to do. The energy is there.'

'I know it's there,' I replied, 'but is that all?'

I set the recording in motion once again. Together we listened to the child's gasp, and the words 'Let go . . . let go . . .'

'Mac,' I said, 'when the child said that, Ken was already dead. Therefore, there could be no further communication between them.'

'Well?'

'How then, after death, can she still identify herself with his personality – a personality that says 'Let go . . . let go . . .' unless . . .

'Unless what?'

'Unless something has happened that we know to be impossible, and what we can see, imprisoned on the screen, is the essence of Ken himself?'

He stared at me, unbelieving, and together we looked once more at the signal, which suddenly took on new meaning, new significance, and as it did so became the expression of our dawning sense of anguish and fear.

'Mac,' I said, 'what have we done?'

Mrs Janus telephoned in the morning to say that Niki had woken up and was acting strangely. She kept throwing herself backwards and forwards. Mrs Janus had tried to quieten her, but nothing she said did any good. No, she had no temperature, she was not feverish. It was this queer rocking movement all the time. She would not eat any breakfast, she would not speak. Could Mac put through the call signal? It might quieten her.

Janus had answered the phone, and we were in the dining-room when he brought us his wife's message. Robbie got up and went to the telephone. He came back again almost immediately.

'I'll go over,' he said. 'What happened yesterday – I should never have allowed it.'

'You knew the risk,' answered Mac. 'We've all known the risk from the very start. You always assured me it would do no harm.'

'I was wrong,' said Robbie. 'Oh, not about the experiment . . . God knows you've done what you wanted to do, and it didn't affect poor Ken one way or the other. He's out of it all now. But I was wrong to let that child become involved.'

'We shouldn't have succeeded without her,' replied Mac.

Robbie went out and we heard him start up the car. Mac and I walked along to the control room. Janus and Robbie had been there before us, and had taken Ken's body away. The room was stripped once more to the essentials of normal routine, with one exception. Charon 3, the storage unit, still functioned as it had done the previous day and through the night, the signal keeping up its steady rise and fall. I found myself glancing at it almost furtively, in the irrational hope that it would cease.

Presently the telephone buzzed, and I answered it. It was Robbie.

'I think we ought to get the child away,' he said at once. 'It looks like catatonic schizophrenia, and whether she becomes violent or not Mrs J. can't cope with it. If Mac will say the word, I could take her up myself to the psychiatric ward at Guy's.'

I beckoned to Mac, explaining the situation. He took the receiver from me.

'Look, Robbie,' he said, 'I'm prepared to take the risk of putting Niki under control. It may work, or it may not.'

The argument continued. I could tell from Mac's gesture of frustration that Robbie would not play. He was surely right. Some irreparable damage might have been done to the child's mind already. Yet, if Robbie did take her up to the hospital, what possible explanation could he give?

Mac waved me over to replace him at the telephone.

'Tell Robbie to stand by,' he said.

I was his subordinate, and could not stop him. He went to the transmitter on Charon 2 and set the control. The call signal was in operation. I lifted the receiver and gave Robbie Mac's message. Then I waited.

I heard Robbie shout to Mrs Janus, 'What's the matter?' – then the sound of the receiver being dropped.

Nothing for a moment or two but distant voices, Mrs Janus, I think, pleading, and then an appeal to Robbie, 'Please, let her try . . .'

Mac went over to Charon 1 and made some adjustments. Then he waved to me to bring the telephone as near to him as it would go, and reached out for the receiver.

'Niki,' he said, 'do you hear me? It's Mac.'

I stood beside him, to catch the whisper from the receiver.

'Yes, Mac.'

She sounded bewildered, even frightened.

'Tell me what's wrong, Niki.'

She began to whimper. 'I don't know. There's a clock ticking somewhere. I don't like it.'

'Where's the clock, Niki?'

She did not answer. Mac repeated his question. I could hear Robbie protest. He must have been standing beside her.

'It's all round,' she said at last. 'It's ticking in my head. Penny doesn't like it either.'

Penny. Who was Penny? Then I remembered. The dead twin.

'Why doesn't Penny like it?'

This was intolerable. Robbie was right. Mac should not put the child through this ordeal. I shook my head at him. He took no notice, but once again repeated his question. I could hear the child burst into tears.

'Penny . . . Ken . . .' she sobbed, 'Penny . . . Ken.'

Instantly Mac switched to the recorded voice of Charon I giving the order on yesterday's programme: 'Stay with Ken. Tell us what happens.'

The child gave a piercing cry, and she must have fallen, because I heard Robbie and Mrs Janus exclaim and the telephone crash.

Mac and I looked at the screen. The rhythm was getting faster, the signal moving in quick jerks. Robbie, at his end, picked up the receiver.

'You'll kill her, Mac,' he called. 'For Christ's sake . . .'

'What's she doing?' asked Mac.

'The same as yesterday,' called Robbie. 'Backwards, forwards, rocking all the time. She's suffocating. Wait . . .'

Once again he must have let the receiver go. Mac switched back to the call signal. The pulsing on the screen was steadying. Then, after a long interval, Robbie's voice came through again.

'She wants to speak,' he said.

There was a pause. The child's voice, expressionless and dull, said, 'Let them go.'

'Are you all right now, Niki?' asked Mac.

'Let them go,' she repeated.

Mac deliberately hung up. Together we watched the signal resume its normal speed.

'Well?' I said. 'What does it prove?'

He looked suddenly old, and immeasurably tired, but there was an expression in his eyes that I had never seen before; a curious, baffled incredulity. It was as though everything he possessed, senses, body, brain, protested and denied the thoughts within.

'It could mean you were right,' he said. 'It could mean survival of intelligence after the body's death. It could mean we've broken through.'

The thought, staggering in its implications, turned us both dumb. Mac recovered first. He went and stood beside Charon 3, his gaze fixed upon the picture.

'You saw it change when the child was speaking,' he said. 'But Niki by herself could not have caused the variation. The power came from Ken's Force Six, and from the dead twin's too. The power is capable of transmission through Niki, but through no one else. Don't you see . . .' He broke off, and swung round to face me, a new excitement dawning. 'Niki is the only link. We must get her here, programme Charon, and put further questions to her. If we really have got intelligence plus power under control . . .'

'Mac,' I interrupted, 'do you want to kill that child, or, worse, condemn her to a mental institution?'

In desperation he looked once more towards the screen. 'I've got to know, Steve,' he said. 'I've got to find out. If intelligence survives, if Force Six can triumph over matter, then it's not just one man who has beaten death but all mankind from the beginning of time. Immortality in some form or other becomes a certainty, the whole meaning of life on earth is changed.'

Yes, I thought, changed forever. The fusion of science and religion in a partnership at first joyous, then the inevitable disenchantment, the scientist realising, and the priest with him, that, with eternity assured, the human being on earth is more easily expendable. Dispatch the maimed, the old, the weak, destroy the very world itself, for what is the point of life if the promise of fulfilment lies elsewhere?

'Mac,' I said, 'you heard what the child said. The words were, "Let them go".'

The telephone rang again. This time it was not Robbie but Janus, from our own extension in the hall. He apologised for disturbing us, but two gentlemen had arrived from the Ministry. He had told them we were in conference, but they said the business was urgent. They had asked to see Mr MacLean at once.

I went into the bar, and the official I had seen in London was standing there with a companion. This first chap expressed apologies, and said the fact was that my predecessor at Saxmere had been to see them, and admitted that his reason for leaving was because he was doubtful of the work MacLean had in progress. There was some experiment going on of which he did not think the Ministry was aware. They wished to speak to MacLean at once.

'He will be with you shortly,' I said. 'In the meantime, if there is anything you want to know, I can brief you.'

They exchanged glances, and then the second chap spoke.

'You're working on vibrations, aren't you,' he asked, 'and their relation to blast? That was what you said in London.'

'We are,' I replied, 'and we have had some success. But, as I warned you, there is still a lot to do.'

'We're here,' he said, 'to be shown what you've achieved.'

'I'm sorry,' I answered, 'the work has been held up since I returned. We've suffered an unfortunate loss on the staff. Nothing to do with the experiment, or the research connected with it. Young Ken Ryan died yesterday from leukaemia.'

Once again there was the swift exchange of glances.

'We heard he was not well,' said the first man. 'Your predecessor told us. In fact, we were given to understand that the experiment in progress was, without the Ministry being informed, connected with this boy's illness.'

'You've been misinformed,' I said. 'His illness had nothing to do with the experiment. The doctor will be back shortly; he can give you the medical details.'

'We should like to see MacLean,' persisted the second chap, 'and we should like to see the electronics department.'

I went back to the control room. I knew that nothing I had said would prevent them from having their way. We were for it. MacLean was standing by Charon 2 doing something to the controls. I looked quickly from him to Charon 3 along-side. The screen was still glowing, but the signal had vanished. I did not say anything, I just stared at him.

'Yes,' he said, 'it's dismantled. I've disconnected every-thing. The force is lost.'

My instantaneous feeling of relief turned to compassion, compassion for the man whose work for months, for years, had gone within five minutes. Destroyed by his own act.

'It isn't finished,' he said, meeting my eyes. 'It's only begun. Oh, one part of it is over. Charon 3 is useless now, and what happened will only be known to the three of us – for Robbie must share our knowledge. We were on the verge of a discov-ery that no one living would believe. But only on the verge. It could well be that both of us were wrong, that what the child told us last night, and again this morning, was simply some distortion of her unconscious mind – I don't know. I just don't know . . . But, because of what she said, I've released the energy. The child is free. Ken is free. He's gone. Where, to what ultimate destination, we shall probably never know. But – and this includes you, Steve, and Robbie, if he will join us – I am prepared to work to the end of my days to find out.'

Then I told him what the officials from the Ministry had said. He shrugged his shoulders.

'I'll tell them all our experiments have failed,' he said, 'that I want to pack in the job. Henceforth, Steve, we'll be on our own. It's strange – somehow I feel nearer to Ken now than I ever did before. Not only Ken, but everyone who has gone before.' He paused, and turned away. 'The child will be all right,' he said. 'Go to her, will you, and send Robbie to me? I'll deal with those sleuths from the Ministry.'

I slipped out of the door at the back and started walking across the marsh towards the coastguard cottages. Cerberus came with me. He was no longer panting, restless, as he had been the night before, but bounded ahead in tearing spirits, returning now and again to make sure that I was following him.

It seemed to me that I had no feeling left, either for what had happened or for what was yet to come. Mac had destroyed, with his own hands, the single thread of evidence that had brought us, through the whole of yesterday, to this morning's dawn. The ultimate dream of every scientist, to give the first answer to the meaning of death, had belonged to us for a brief few hours. We had captured the energy, the energy had ignited the spark, and from that point on there had appeared to loom world after world of discovery.

Now . . . now, my faith was waning. Perhaps we had been wrong, tricked by our own emotions and the suffering of a frightened, backward child. The ultimate questions would never receive their answer, either from us or from anyone.

The marsh fell back on either side of me, and I climbed the scrubby hill to the coastguard cottages. The dog ran on ahead, barking. Away to the right, outlined on the cliff edge, the damned U.S. cadets were blowing their bugles once again.

The raucous, discordant screeches tore the air. They were trying, of all things, to sound the Reveille.

I saw Robbie come out of the Januses' cottage, and the child was with him. She seemed all right. She ran forward to greet the dog. Then she heard the sound of the Reveille, and lifted her arms. As the tempo increased she swayed to the rhythm, and ran out towards the cliffs with her arms above her head, laughing, dancing, the dog barking at her feet. The cadets looked back, laughing with her; and then there was nothing else but the dog barking, the child dancing, and the sound of those thin, high bugles in the air.